PERSONAL FILE:

Name: Mina Snotbridge a.k.a Mina Mistry

Occupation: Student at Greenville Elementary

Best Friend: Mr Panda

Second Best Friend: Holly Loafer

Distinguishing Features: Extreme intelligence and ambition. Destined to become a private investigator

Hobbies:

Playing the cello,

investigating

mysteries and

spying on people

LOG ENTRY #1

Location: My bedroom
Status: General life update

It's been a while since I've written an update, but then it's been a while since I've had a hot case to investigate. And **HOT** really is the word: the summer holidays started last week and Greenville is in the middle of a heatwave. I'm not complaining though. Granny Meera has been experimenting with lots of new ice cream recipes and some of them are great!

She's definitely onto something with the creamy mango and chocolate chip. The vanilla, banana and blackcurrant is excellent, and the custard and cinnamon is actually amazing! Unfortunately, there are a few others that need some work. The black olive, grape and caramelised onion flavour really needs a rethink. And although the idea of

combining pizza and ice cream might sound
good in theory, the truth is that tomato ice
cream drizzled with melted cheese and
topped with chunks of anchovy tastes …
well, it tastes about as good as it sounds.

Still, it is nice to have some time off school, even though I'm never actually at home.

Mum and Dad both work away a lot. Dad works for the Ministry of Transport (or so he claims ... I have a theory that he's actually a spy) and Mum travels around the world, inspecting factories.

This means I end up sleeping over at Granny Meera's a lot and spending lots of time at Holly's.

Holly Loafer is my best friend (well, second best after Mr Panda).

Spending time with Holly usually consists of receiving a suspicious invitation like "Why don't you come over and we'll watch a documentary?" or "Let's prepare for the English test together," and then spending most of the day watching Holly try on clothes.

Sometimes people think it's strange that we're best friends, considering how **DIFFERENT** we are.

Mina:

- Likes crime investigation dramas
- Plays the cello in the school band

- Idea of fun is helping Granny Meera cook and bake
- Likes to keep detailed files on everyone she knows (including friends and family) in case they should ever be under suspicion of committing a crime

Holly:

- Can spend up to two hours choosing the right shade of lip gloss
- Wants to win Teen Talent and become a celebrity
- Is in love with Gareth Trumpshaw (eww!!)
- Once refused to get on a bus because it clashed with her shoes

- Spends hours going through shopping websites and making spreadsheets listing all the different upcoming trends in handbags (Honestly, I don't understand it. Surely there are much better things Holly could be doing with her time?)

Granny Meera says that we're more alike than we realise, but I don't know where she's looking. Sometimes, I don't even think we're on the same planet!

Anyway, last Friday I was at Holly's house, and we were sitting at the kitchen table making bead necklaces. Well, *I* was

making a bead necklace. Holly seemed to

be making an entire jewellery collection to

coordinate with her summer wardrobe.

Holly's mum was going through her papers in the living room. She's a lecturer at the local university, so she was preparing things for next term. She kept nipping in and out of the kitchen to charge her phones or to get a cup of coffee.

Well, that's what Holly said she was doing.

For all I know, Holly and her mum have

their own secret language. I mean, over

the course of the afternoon Holly's mum

asked if we wanted a flat white, a long

black and a triple mocha Al Pacino! I didn't

know what any of these things meant. But

she did ask me while hovering around the

coffee machine, so I deduced they were

all varieties of coffee and said no. I've tried

it before and I'm not making that mistake

again - **iT'S DiSGUSTiNG!**

PERSONAL FILE:

Name: Lucille Loafer (married to Kurt Loafer; mother to Holly Loafer)

Occupation: College Professor

Distinguishing Features: Looks like an older version of Holly, and has two mobile phones

Hobbies: Protesting, telling people they're wrong and ordering mind-bendingly complicated coffees

Holly was just telling me that Gareth Trumpshaw had started using a new kind of hair gel, when her mum came into the kitchen again.

'How are you girls doing?' she asked. 'I'm just rushed off my feet today … go, go, go!'

She looked down at our handiwork. Holly had created a collection of accessories which would coordinate with her bags, shoes and sunglasses. I'd made a long string with random beads on it.

'Oh Mina!' Holly's mum said brightly.

'Look at your necklace, it's so … tasteful!'

Holly looked up at her in disbelief.

'TASTEFUL?! Are you serious, Mum? It's hideous! Sorry Mina, but fashion is not your thing.'

I took a look at my handiwork. It wasn't a patch on Holly's, but calling it hideous seemed a bit harsh.

'I don't think it's my best work,' I offered.

'Well, I would wear it,' said Holly's mum firmly.

Holly and I shared a meaningful look.

Then Holly picked up the necklace and

handed it to her mum, who put it on and

walked off delightedly.

'Sorry about that,' said Holly, 'she's so

EMBARRASSING.'

I nodded. 'It's ok. I think she just wants people to like her.'

As Holly and I continued making jewellery, we could hear her mum on the phone in the living room. She was shouting down the phone at someone.

'What's up with your mum, anyway?' I asked. 'She seems pretty cross about something.'

Holly rolled her eyes. 'I don't know. She's probably upset about something to do with rights ... or politics ... or ... No, I'll be honest: I have no idea. Are you coming skating at the weekend?'

I do enjoy skating, but this weekend I actually had plans (for once). Mum was in town and she'd promised to take me to my cousins' birthday party.

'I can't go on Saturday,' I told Holly. 'It's Mahesh and Maheshwari's birthday party.'

'Whose birthday?' Holly asked.

'The twins – my cousins, remember?'

'Oh yeah!' said Holly. 'Anyway,' she breezed on, 'don't worry, we're all meeting on Sunday afternoon. Danny and Percy will be there and, most importantly, Gareth will be there. So you can't let me down. I can't let him see me on my own.'

I raised an eyebrow. 'Why not?'

'Because he needs to know that I'm really popular, of course,' said Holly.

I couldn't follow Holly's logic. I didn't see how hanging around with *me* was

going to send the message that she's really popular. But then, Holly seems to be the **EXPERT** when it comes to boys … Well, she's more of an expert than me, at least. To be honest, I'm not really very interested in them.

Holly's mum walked back into the kitchen, on her way to get a flapuccino or something, and overheard Holly talking about Gareth. I don't think that Holly's mum likes Gareth very much. Not a lot of people do, except for Holly.

'You're not going on about that

TRUMPSHAW BOY again,

are you?' Holly's mum sighed.

Holly put her hands on her hips. 'I don't

understand what you have against Gareth,

Mum. He's clever and

good-looking–'

'Oh, no,' Holly's

mum cut in, 'I've

got nothing against

him. He's just a bit …

bland. Why don't you

look for someone with a different culture; someone you can learn from?' She looked straight at me. 'Mina, do you have any cousins?'

This threw me a bit. I wondered whether Holly's mum thought it was part of my "culture" to have a catalogue of prospective girlfriends and boyfriends ready, in case I needed to arrange a marriage at the last minute!

'Well, I have two cousins, Mahesh and Maheshwari,' I said. 'They're **TWiNS**, but one of them is a girl and they're about to turn seven. It's their birthday this weekend. I'm going to their **PARTY** on Saturday.'

'Oh, you're having a party?' said Holly's mum. 'I didn't know if you celebrated that sort of thing in your community.'

Feeling awkward, I stared back at her. 'Err ... We do in my family. I thought everyone did, but I'm not an expert on birthdays.'

Holly looked at her mum as if she were **REALLY** embarrassing herself. 'Mina's from *our* community Mum,' she said 'and, believe me, there's nothing interesting

about her!'

I had to admire Holly, not many people

had the ability to **DeFeND** you and

iNSULT you in the same sentence.

LOG ENTRY #2

Location: Auntie Nayna and
Uncle Dee's house
Status: Digesting party food

I'd been looking forward to the twins'

birthday party. The whole family was going

to be there. Well, apart from Dad who'd

told us he was working in London for two

weeks. I suspected that he'd been sent on a **SECRET MISSION**.

Dad claims to work for the Ministry of Transport, but I know that's just a cover story. In real life he's a secret agent who travels around the world catching villains and solving mysteries.

Fortunately, Mum was back from India, so I'd get to spend some time with her. She had been inspecting a factory out there, and it felt like she had been away for ages. Mum travels a lot for work, and even when she's not at work she's usually on the phone to work.

PERSONAL FILE:

Name: Chameli Mistry-Snotbridge (married to Charles Snotbridge; mother to Mina Snotbridge)

Occupation: Manager at a toy factory

Distinguishing Features: Very pretty but very serious, wears a suit, and is usually at work or on the phone to work. Likes to be in charge and tends to take over when something needs to be organised

Hobbies: She doesn't have time for hobbies

Mum and I pulled up into Auntie Nayna and Uncle Dee's drive and parked behind Granny Meera's neon yellow van, which she had parked partly on the drive and partly across the flower bed, with one wheel overhanging the fish pond. The party was clearly underway. As we approached the front door, I could hear loud music and kids giggling and shouting.

There were trays of food everywhere.
Granny Meera had been hard at work.

There seemed to be different things going
on all over the house. As we walked through
the door, a stampede of children with tiger
faces ran past us, suggesting that there was
face painting going on somewhere. I could
smell spices and burning charcoal, so there
must have been a barbecue in the back
garden. There was music blasting from an
improvised salon in the living room, where
Auntie Nayna was cutting someone's hair

and spraying the ends green. Auntie Nayna

is Mum's sister, but they're very different to

each other!

PERSONAL FILE:

Name: Auntie Nayna (mum's sister; married to Uncle Dee; mother to my twin cousins Mahesh and Maheshwari)

Occupation: Hairdresser and make-up artist for TV shows like Teen Talent

Distinguishing Features: Really lively, loves to party, loves fashion and music

Hobbies: Doing hair and make-up at parties, for fun

Another group of seven-year-olds ran past me on their way to the garden. Two of them had red hair, one had purple, one had blue and one had orange. I had a feeling Auntie Nayna was going to have a lot of explaining to do when the kids' parents came to pick them up.

Auntie Nayna smiled at me and yelled: 'Just 17 all wear their hair like this. They're all the rage; the kids love them!'

I nodded. I'm not really into pop music, but I had heard of Just 17. Holly was a

BiG fan. Then I shouted back, 'Where are the twins?'

Auntie Nayna mouthed something, but I couldn't hear her too well over the loud music. She seemed to point in the direction of the garden, so I made my way out the door before she could offer me a haircut.

The party would definitely be going on in the back garden too. This was what normally happened at my aunt and uncle's parties. Auntie Nayna is a party animal and Uncle Dee is quiet and chilled out. So Uncle

Dee usually takes care of the barbecue in the garden or helps Granny Meera in the kitchen, while Auntie Nayna usually has a disco and does hair and makeup in the living room. Everyone else just moves around between them.

When I got to the garden, I found Granny Meera looking after the barbecue while Uncle Dee was surrounded by a circle of children sat on the grass. Granny Meera was now sporting a bright red Mohican.

'Hi Granny, nice hair!'

Granny Meera grinned back at me. 'Hello Pumpkin! Thank you, I let your Auntie Nayna practise on me. She's doing the hair and make-up for some pop video next week.'

'Well, it really suits you,' I said, and I meant it. 'It definitely goes with your van.'

Granny Meera smiled at my awkward compliment.

'What's Uncle Dee doing?' I asked, noticing that Uncle Dee had brought out a big mysterious object covered with a piece of cloth.

'You don't want to miss this!' replied Granny Meera. 'Your Uncle Dee has been very busy. He's prepared a special birthday show with Princess. Go and have a look!'

Princess was Uncle Dee's pride and joy: his pet parrot. Uncle Dee had owned Princess for years, and he'd spent hours teaching her tricks. I went to sit next to Mahesh and Maheshwari and watch the rest of the show.

'And for our next trick ...' Uncle Dee announced, 'Princess will eat maggots straight out of my ears!'

All the kids screamed 'Eww!' and 'Ugh!' as they watched the trick.

Uncle Dee took a bow. 'Thank you, thank you! And now, for the grand finale …' He paused and put on a Just 17 song. The twins looked really excited.

'That's our favourite song!'

Princess the parrot started to nod her head and sing along to Just 17's latest hit "Glowstick It".

Uncle Dee grabbed a nearby bag and started handing out glowsticks. We

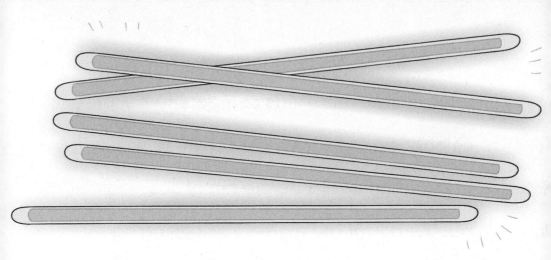

all danced along as Princess the parrot

performed the song.

Holly was going to be so jealous when

I told her about the party, with its Just 17

hairdos and Princess the parrot performing

their song. Just 17 are famous for winning

last year's edition of Young Talent. It's a TV

45

talent show where kids compete to become celebrities, and it's Holly's dream to win it one day. I may not be big fan of Just 17, but the parrot did a great job of singing the song. **I thought that it was way better than the original.**

At the end of the song, Princess said 'Happy Birthday Mahesh and Maheshwari!'. Then she said, 'Turn around now.'

We all turned around. Auntie Nayna, Mum and Granny Meera were carrying a huge cake.

'Now twins!' said Auntie Nayna. 'This year we've all decided to get you two big presents, instead of lots of little ones. Come and blow out the candles on your cake and make a wish!'

Mahesh started to say: 'Ooh!! I hope it's …'

But then Maheshwari shushed him.

We all sang happy birthday as the twins walked up to the cake, closed their eyes and blew out the candles. Then we all cheered!

Uncle Dee brought out two huge boxes and the twins' eyes lit up. The boxes had been tied with lots of string and ribbon, and the twins had to cut through it all to get the boxes open. Finally, they managed it. There, under all the string and cardboard were **TWO BEAUTIFUL BRAND-NEW BICYCLES**. The twins were really excited. For a moment I thought they were

going to jump on their bikes and ride off into the distance, leaving two bicycle-shaped holes in the garden fence.

'That's not all …' said Auntie Nayna with a grin.

Mahesh and Maheshwari turned to look at her, eyes wide. 'It's not?'

'It's not!' she told them. 'Get ready for a road trip, because we've got tickets to go and see Just 17 live at the Soggy Fields Festival in Rainy Valley tomorrow night!!

At this point the twins just started

bouncing and screaming with excitement. It was great to see them looking so happy! And a relief not to have to chase them and their new bicycles down the road.

Now that the presents had been unwrapped, everybody crowded around Granny Meera to get some cake. I waited until all the other guests had been served. When I finally got to the front of the queue, Granny Meera looked like she was **DYING TO TELL ME SOMETHING**.

'What's up?' I asked her. 'You look like you're about to burst.'

Granny Meera gave me a furtive smile. 'Well, I wasn't going to tell you, but …'

'… but you can't keep a secret for more than five minutes without your head exploding,' I finished for her.

'I've been hired to do the catering for the opening of the new bike park next week!' she yelled excitedly. Then she lost all her words and just started screaming. **'EEEEEEK!!!!'**

Granny Meera grabbed me and started **JUMPiNG** up and down.

I jumped with her, but, truthfully, I had no idea what she was talking about. 'What bike park opening?'

Granny Meera stared at me. 'Haven't you heard? It's all that the town has been talking about! They're opening a **BRAND-NEW** skate and bike park for you kids next week. There's going to be a competition to see who has the best customised bike, skateboard or scooter. And there's a competition for the best rider too. The Mayor will award each winner with a **MYSTERIOUS GRAND PRIZE**. He'll also be announcing the winner of Greenville's annual environmental awareness competition. It's all very exciting!'

I blinked. 'Really? Wow!' I usually stay on top of the local news – well, I flick through the newspaper to check for any recent crimes – so it surprised me that I hadn't heard about this.

Granny Meera was still talking, '… and I'll be doing the food. Isn't that great? I think it will be nice for you young people to have somewhere to go and hang out. A place that's not overrun with wrinklies.'

She winked at me and I smiled. Granny Meera had a point. The roller rink was pretty much the only place that we have to hang out, but at the weekends it's full of teachers and parents. **IT'S AWFUL!** They completely take over. They have a roller disco and we have to listen to **THEiR** music. They're always saying things like "No misbehaving, I have my eyes on you!" or "If you carry on playing 'who can stuff the most crisps into their mouth in one minute', I'll have to tell your parents."

So Greenville is getting a new skate park? Sounds like great news!

LOG ENTRY #3

Location: Outside the roller rink

Status: Suffering from smoke inhalation

I went to meet Holly at the roller rink at four o'clock on Sunday afternoon. It was pretty busy. There's not that much else for kids to do in Greenville in the summer.

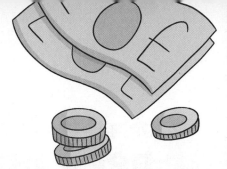

Curly Greg was at the door. I scratched around in my pocket for the **THREE-POUND ENTRY FEE** and handed it to him. He gave me a plastic bracelet to prove that I'd paid, then went back to tend his shop. I made my way over to the rink. The sparkly bracelet made me feel like I'd just walked into a festival.

I like the roller rink, although it is in need of some updating. It opened in 1975 when disco music was popular. To put that into perspective: **MY DAD HADN'T BEEN BORN YET!** Granny Meera used to come to the roller rink with Grandad, but that was a long time ago. Granny Meera hasn't been interested in roller skating since she discovered kiteboarding.

The roller rink is a family business. Curly Greg started running it when his mum, Curly Sandra retired. As well as the roller rink, Greg has a little shop where he sells bikes and skates, and carries out repairs.

I spotted Danny Dingle and Percy McDuff as I walked in. Bill Crisp from orchestra was also there. Bill plays the tuba, and the interesting thing about him is that he takes his tuba **EVERYWHERE**. This makes him very easy to spot at a distance, although it doesn't improve his chances of ever getting a girlfriend.

I sat on a bench to change into my skates.

A blonde blur whizzed past (I assumed that it was Gareth Trumpsaw), followed by another blur with long blonde hair that smelt of perfume (I assumed that was Holly chasing after him). Percy and Danny had now moved over to one end of the rink and were poking at something with screwdrivers.

I finished lacing up my skates and started to carefully

make my way around the rink, staying close to the sides. I mean, I'm okay on roller skates but I'm better on a scooter. I suppose that was another good reason to look forward to the new bike park opening: I'd have somewhere fun to ride my scooter.

IT WAS REALLY BUSY. There were lots of other kids from school there, and unfortunately it was also full of teachers and parents. I saw Holly on the other side of the rink, so I started making my way towards her. Immediately, I was

nearly knocked down by Mr Hammond the

science teacher, who was being chased by

Ms Mills, our terrifying PE teacher.

Soooooryyyyyy ...

I'd only just got my balance back when Gareth's Dad flew past me – missing me by an inch. Seconds later, Danny's Dad rolled straight into me.

Loook oooouuut!!!!!!

He'd only just helped me to my feet when someone put on some **AWFUL** disco music. All the grown-ups piled into the centre of the rink and started dancing and generally being really **EMBARRASSiNG**. Holly and a group of other kids had moved to one side of the roller rink, so I carefully skated around the outside of the rink towards them. It was the longest way around, but by far the safest.

Gareth Trumpshaw was the first to notice my arrival. He looked flustered. 'Hi Mina! You look–' he began before Holly interrupted him.

'Hi Mina, are you okay?' she said.

'Hi guys,' I said. 'Yeah, I'm okay. I can't believe how the grown-ups behave on Roller Disco Sunday. They'd never let us behave like that!'

At that point Mr Norton the headmaster whizzed past, wearing a ruffled shirt and extremely tight mustard-yellow flares.

As we watched, there was a loud ripping sound and they split right **ACROSS THE BUM**. I looked away. Nobody needed to see that.

I'd never seen Holly look more unimpressed. 'I've just seen our headmaster's underpants,' she said faintly.

Gareth looked shell-shocked. 'Little ducks …' he muttered, still staring.

I put my hands on my hips. 'I can't wait for the skate park to open. We really don't deserve this.'

Gareth shook himself and rejoined the conversation. 'Are you guys going to enter the competitions on the opening day?' he asked. 'I've been working on modifying my scooter.'

'I've already customised my skates,' Holly chimed in.

I realised that everybody was way ahead of me. 'I hadn't thought about it,' I said. 'I might see if my cousins want to customise their bikes. They got new ones for their birthday, yesterday.'

Just then Percy and Danny rolled up,

screwdrivers in hand.

'Hi!' I called over cheerfully. 'What are the

screwdrivers for?'

Danny grinned back at us. 'We were just

fixing the smoke machine. What are you all

chatting about?'

'We're talking about the new skate and

bike park that's about to open. Gareth

has already modified his scooter and

Holly has customised her skates. There's a

competition for the best custom job.'

Danny glanced intensely at Gareth.

UH OH ... maybe I shouldn't have

mentioned the competition.

Danny and Gareth don't

really get on and they have

to compete at **everything**.

'Oh, we've customised our scooters,' Danny replied. 'They're awesome and fearsome and they're going to … They're going to … What are they going to do again, Percy?'

Danny nudged Percy to get him to go along with the pretence, but Percy hadn't really been listening. 'Oh!' he said. 'Do you want to come over to work on your scooter with us next week, Mina?'

I thought about it for a moment. 'Okay,' I agreed, 'I should probably make an effort.'

Gareth frowned. 'I thought you said you'd already customised your scooters.'

'Yes,' said Danny, staring at Gareth like a cat in a fight, 'but we're just missing a few finishing touches to make them even more **SUPER FEARSOME**.'

As Danny said this, there was a crackle followed by an explosion. The roller rink started to fill up with smoke. We could hear people skating and bashing into each other.

The DJ stopped the music as the fire alarm

came on.

'Okay,' said Mr Norton crossly stumbling

through the **SMOKE**. 'Who's the

SMARTY PANTS who has

been fiddling with the smoke machine?'

These were his last words before his trousers fell down completely and got tangled up with Bill Crisp's tuba, dragging both Bill and his tuba into the dense smoke.

'Let's get out of here,' said Holly. 'We can talk outside.'

Danny nodded frantically. 'Yeah, before they end up blaming one of us for this accident!'

LOG ENTRY #4

Location: My bedroom
Status: On a mission

It was just after six when I got home.

Holly's mum dropped me off. She was still

wearing that ugly bead necklace I had

cobbled together on Friday.

I went straight to the kitchen, where I

found two notes on the fridge:

Note 1:

16.10 - Just had to rush off to the office. I've made you some sandwiches and I bought Mr Panda his favourite crisps.
See you later! Mum xxx

I looked over to the kitchen counter

where I saw two packets of salt and vinegar

Hula Hoops.

Note 2:

16.16 – Call your cousins! xx

I grabbed a sandwich and a packet

of Hula Hoops and went upstairs to my

room, to find Mr Panda. I swung open my

bedroom door and Mr Panda looked up

from his paragliding magazine. His eye lit
up when he saw that I had brought him his
favourite crisps.

'Don't bother getting up, just enjoy your crisps,' I told him. 'I just have to go and call Mahesh and Maheshwari. They were supposed to be at a concert this evening, so I hope everything is okay …'

It *was* strange that they'd be back home so soon. They were supposed to be watching Just 17 at the Soggy Fields festival in Rainy Valley.

I called and Auntie Nayna picked up.

'Oh hello …' she said. 'Mina, the twins are both very upset. They want to speak to you.'

Auntie Nayna passed the phone to Mahesh. In the background I heard Maheshwari say: '**MUM!** Leave the room. This is a private conversation, alright?'

I heard a door shut, then Mahesh spoke.

'Mina, we need your help,' he said.

'What happened?' I asked. 'I thought you were supposed to be at the Just 17 concert.'

I heard Maheshwari trying to get to the phone.

'It was a **DiSASTeR**-' she began.

Mahesh took over. 'It was a disaster, Mina.

We drove all the way to Rainy Valley, but when we got to the town entrance we were turned away by police.'

'Tell her about the rain,' Maheshwari said in the background.

'Apparently it rained all night last night,' Mahesh continued. 'As the festival was in the middle of the valley, the stage and all the tents got **WASHED AWAY** by mud slides.'

My jaw dropped. 'Oh my goodness! Was anybody hurt?'

'Nobody important,' said Mahesh dismissively. 'Luckily, Just 17 hadn't arrived yet, and they're the only band we like. That's not why we called you, though.'

'IT'S NOT?'

Mahesh lowered his voice. 'We need your help with something … **TOP SECReT**.'

As far as they knew, I was just a normal girl. I was a bit surprised that they would think that I would be the best person to help them out. Or that they would have any problems worthy of a **SECReT MiSSiON**.

'Tell her, tell her that we know her secret,' Maheshwari chimed in.

I was shocked. I couldn't be 100%

sure if they were talking about my secret identity as an **UNDERCOVER DETECTIVE**. But I couldn't risk them talking about it on the phone. After all, the line might be tapped.

'Okay, I'm on it,' I cut them off. 'Tell me what you need.'

Mahesh started talking immediately. 'Mina, something terrible has happened: our bikes have been **STOLEN**.'

I couldn't believe my ears.

'Are you sure?'

'Yes, completely,' he replied.

Maheshwari was talking in the background again. 'Tell her about how, when we got back, they had **DISAPPEARED** from the garage,' she said.

'They just disappeared!' Mahesh explained. 'We'd left them in the garage and they were gone when we got back.'

I narrowed my eyes. This *was* a mystery.

'And nobody knows anything?' I asked.

'We don't know,' said Mahesh sheepishly. 'Mum and Dad said we couldn't play with them until next week. Dad wants to teach

us to ride without stabilisers, once the new

skatepark is open.'

Maheshwari grabbed the phone. 'But we

didn't see why we couldn't play with them

in the garage. And *someone* forgot to lock the garage door.

Mahesh sounded indignant in the background. 'Hey, that's not fair! You could have checked too!'

'Anyway,' Maheshwari continued, 'when we got back, **THE BiKES WERE GONE**. Can you help us find them before Mum and Dad realise and ground us forever?'

I promised Mahesh and Maheshwari that I would go over to their house in the morning and start looking into it straight away. Then I hung up the phone and went back to my room, to explain the case to **MR PANDA**.

He listened carefully and we started drawing up a plan for our investigation.

The first things we needed to do were: investigate the crime scene, question the witnesses (if there were any), and see if the perpetrators had left any clues. I would also have to draw up a list of suspects to **INTERROGATE**.

Since we couldn't do anything else on the list yet, Mr Panda and I decided to start thinking about **SUSPECTS**.

Anyone in Greenville could have the motive to steal two new bicycles – especially with the opening of the skate

park just around the corner – so we
decided to start with people who knew
about the bikes.

SUSPECTS

- My whole family

- Everyone who was at the party

- Anyone who any of those guests told

I looked at the list – it wasn't very helpful. It still added up to pretty much **everyone** in Greenville.

I decided that I could rule out my family. After all, everyone had worked together to buy the bikes, so it wouldn't make sense for any of us to steal them. That left me with a suspect list of: every person in Greenville who wasn't a member of my family. **GREAT**.

Next, I began ruling out the people I'd told about the bikes. I'd already arranged

to go to Danny's house in the morning,

to work on customising our scooters, so I

would start there.

Mr Panda went back to reading his

magazine and I gazed out of the window.

At that moment, I saw a man in a spacesuit

riding a skateboard down the street.

I thought I might be hallucinating. I rubbed

my eyes and then checked

the inside of my sandwich

to make sure the bacon

hadn't gone mouldy …

No … there he was again! A grown man in a

spacesuit, skating past my window.

LOG ENTRY #5

Location: Auntie Nayna and Uncle Dee's house
Status: Investigating

I arrived at Mahesh and Maheshwari's house at ten o'clock on Monday morning. The twins were waiting for me at the front window and they rushed to the door before I could ring the doorbell.

'Mina, Mina!!' they chorused. 'We're so glad you're here!'

'Don't worry,' I told them, 'I'm here to help. Let's get to the bottom of this … I need to see where the bikes were stolen from.'

The twins led me towards the garage. I had a look around.

'The bikes were parked there,' said Mahesh. He sighed, pointing at an **EMPTY SPACE** in the garage.

I looked closely at the empty space. 'So, when was the last time you saw the bikes?'

'On Sunday morning, just before we left,' the twins replied together.

I opened my notebook. 'And who was here on Sunday?'

Maheshwari thought for a moment. 'Dad left to go and visit a friend in the morning,' she said, 'then Mum, Mahesh and I left to go to Rainy Valley. We left at about ten.'

'When we got back at four in the afternoon, the bikes weren't here,' Mahesh added.

'Nobody had come back home,' said Mahesh worriedly.

'And the garage door was left unlocked?' I asked.

'Yes,' replied Mahesh.

I looked around the garage for clues. Although the thief didn't have to break in to steal the bikes, they still must have known that everybody would be out at **EXACTLY THOSE TIMES**, and that the bikes were in the garage.

Everybody who was at the party knew about the bikes. They also knew that the twins would be away until Monday. But how many people knew that Uncle Dee would be out too? Maybe I couldn't rule out the family after all.

As I looked around, something small and bright caught my eye: **A STRAND OF BRIGHT RED HAIR**. I carefully picked it up and wrapped it in a clean tissue. As I did so, I noticed that some red had come off onto my fingers. It must

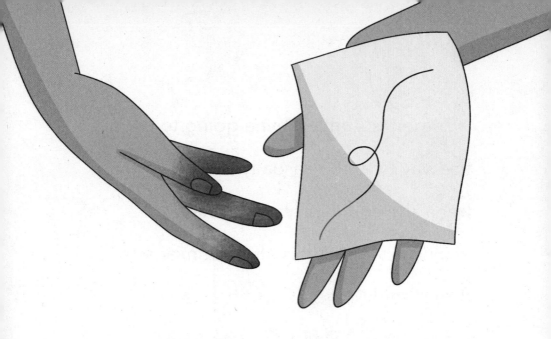

have been recently dyed. **MY FiRST REAL CLUe!**

I promised the twins to be in touch as soon as I had news. I knew I'd have to find a way of **INTeRROGATiNG** the family, but I'd have to be discreet.

'When is Auntie Nayna going to be in, by the way?' I asked casually. 'I wanted to ask her if she could just trim my hair.'

'She'll be back this afternoon, at about three,' said Maheshwari.

I nodded. 'Okay, I'll call her later.'

The twins looked sad as I made my way out. It's hardly surprising: first their concert was demolished by a giant mudslide, then their new bicycles got stolen. The only person I knew with a **WORSE** birthday story was Percy. Last year he was given a tennis set. Only minutes after unwrapping it, he ran face first into a cactus while chasing a tennis ball. Then he turned around with his eyes shut and stepped onto a rake – the handle shot up and hit him square between the eyes. Then, as his mum was pulling the spines out of his face with some tweezers, she told him off for leaving the rake lying around in the garden.

'Please don't worry,' I told them. 'We'll catch the thief. You'll get your bikes back, you'll see.'

I was about to walk out through the front door when I heard someone talking in the living room. 'Quick, get them in the van … get them in the van!'

I poked my head through the doorway. Princess the parrot stared back at me, repeating 'Get them in the van!' over and over again.

So, the good news for my **INVESTIGATION** was that I had found a witness. The bad news was that my only witness was a talking **PARROT**.

LOG ENTRY #6

Location: My bedroom

Status: Collecting clues

It was only a twenty-minute scoot through town from the twins' house to Danny's. I'd arranged to meet Danny and Percy so we could **CUSTOMISE** our scooters together. Danny and Percy's

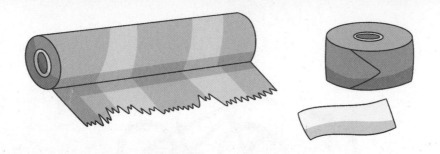

decorating skills tended to involve a lot of **STiCKY TAPe** and **TiNFOiL**, but they were still better than me at this sort of thing. The last thing I made was that bead necklace that Holly's mum is still wearing. It makes her look like she's being strangled by a dying caterpillar.

Danny's mum let me in. She told me that the boys were already in the **CLUBHOUSe**.

'Sorry about the mess in the back garden,' she said. 'The boys have been banned from the house until it's cleaned up.'

I opened the kitchen door onto the back garden and I was met with an image from a science fiction film. There were bits of metal, old wheels and pieces of … of **STUFF** everywhere. It looked as though a satellite had crashed onto the lawn. I navigated my way around the wreckage and made my way up the tree to the **CLUBHOUSE**.

I knocked on the trunk and called up. 'Hello, it's Mina! Your mum said to come straight up.'

Danny poked his head out of the trapdoor. 'Hi Mina, come in!'

'Your mum told me that you've been banned from going back indoors until you clean up the mess in the garden,' I said. 'What happened?'

Danny sighed. 'Yeah, I know … and that's not even our mess! Dad's been working on an invention for the skate park opening.

An invention to blow everyone's minds, he said. Apparently he's in competition with Gareth's dad again.'

'What's the invention?' I asked.

'I can't tell you,' said Danny. **'IT'S TOP SECRET.'**

Percy chimed in. 'But we can tell you that he's needed to borrow bits from most of the machines and appliances in Danny's house.'

I frowned. Danny's dad had a habit of 'borrowing' people's belongings when he was working on an invention. I made a mental note to see if I could spot any bicycle wheels.

Danny and Percy beckoned me towards the clubhouse window and started pointing at things.

'That's what's left of the toaster …' said Danny.

'AND, OH, LOOK!' Percy nudged Danny. 'That was your mum's exercise bike.'

'Yeah,' Danny chuckled, 'and I think bits of that were the microwave.'

Percy pointed. 'And in that corner, over there, is what's left of Danny's skateboard.'

'Yeah,' Danny nodded, then his face fell.

'What?!! ... Really????!!!!' I said.

'Danny's dad has been going through all the bins and skips in town too,' Percy explained. 'He's trying to find the missing parts for his invention.'

Danny nodded. 'And, unfortunately, every missing part seems to come attached to lots of other useless parts, which is why the garden looks like a scrap yard ...'

'... which is why Danny's mum is making Danny's dad sleep in the shed,' Percy finished for him.

Something didn't quite add up. 'I still don't understand why you guys have been banished to the garden if the mess is all your dad's,' I said to Danny.

'I think it's because Danny's mum thinks we're a **BAD iNFLUENCE** on his dad,' said Percy.

I thought for a minute, then nodded.

THAT MADE SENSE.

Then, before I could get any more

sidetracked, I thought I'd tell Percy and

Danny about the missing bikes, just in case

they knew anything.

'You'll never guess what has happened–,'

I began.

Percy immediately interrupted me. 'I love

this game! Err … Miss Quimby fell asleep

with her face in a bowl of chocolate icing

and woke up thinking that she's finally eaten

so many **DOUGHNUTS** that she's turned into one!'

I looked at him. 'Err … no.'

'Oh!' said Danny. 'My turn! Ms Mills, the fearsome PE teacher, has a twin brother, and they sometimes swap identities and nobody notices.'

I had to think about that one. It was an interesting theory. 'Maybe …' I said finally, 'but that's not what I was going to say. Remember how I told you about my cousins getting new bikes for their birthday?'

'Yes,' Percy nodded.

At the same time, Danny shook his head and said, 'No?'

'Well,' I sighed, 'they've been stolen!'

'That's terrible!' Percy gasped. 'Who would do something like that?'

I shrugged. 'I don't know. But if you hear anything or see any kids with new bikes, let me know, okay?'

Danny and Percy agreed to keep an eye

out for anything **SUSPICIOUS**, although I wasn't sure how much help they would be. I mean, Danny didn't even notice that his dad had **DISMANTLED** his skateboard and left bits of it right under his nose. Still, I needed all the help I could get.

'Right, so the scooters,' I said, changing the subject, '… Do you have any ideas?'

Danny and Percy looked at each other as if they were very pleased with themselves.

'You're going to love this, Mina,' Percy told me.

Danny cleared the table with one sweeping motion and laid out the design he'd been working on.

'I'm not sure I get it,' I admitted after a moment of looking at it.

'The idea is that we all customise our scooters with one common theme,' said Percy.

'Okay, what's the theme?' I asked.

Percy's expression lit up. **'TINFOIL!!'**

Danny spread his arms out dramatically. 'And **FIRE!!!**'

No surprises there, then!

I summoned a smile. 'Okay, well, shall we start with the tin foil and just assume that the fire will appear on its own, by accident, like it usually does?

Before I left, I had another look at the scrapheap in Danny's garden. I couldn't see **ANY BiKe PARTS**, but it was impossible to be sure. I sighed. Well, I was going to have to meet up again with Danny and Percy to put the finishing touches to my scooter anyway, so I'd get another chance to look then.

It was about three o'clock when I got home. A lot of the bits of foil I'd stuck on my scooter had come flying off on the way home, so I had even more of an excuse to go back. I went to the fridge to grab a snack and saw a note Mum had stuck there:

Mina! Call Gareth Trumpshaw, he says it's important. xx

HOW STRANGE! Why would Gareth call me? I thought for a moment. Gareth's dad was just as competitive as Danny's and even more ruthless. Could Gareth's dad be the bike thief? I couldn't imagine what Gareth might want, but I knew it could be useful to talk to him. Maybe he knew what his dad was up to; it was worth a shot.

I called him back, but Gareth wouldn't say what he wanted. In the end, we arranged to meet in town at eleven the next day. Then I called Auntie Nayna to ask her to trim my hair. I planned to go over there after

meeting Gareth.

After sorting all that out, I went up to

my room. Mr Panda was on my computer,

watching videos about white-water rafting.

I didn't like interrupting him, but I had important updates on the case.

Three very important clues had turned up:

Clue 1

The first clue was the bright red hair I had found in the garage. Auntie Nayna had been dying people's hair red at the party. So the hair must have got into the garage between Saturday afternoon and Sunday afternoon.

Clue 2

Another important thing was our witness statement. Princess the parrot had said "Quick, get them in the van". So we knew the theft was not carried out by kids acting alone. An adult must have loaded the bicycles into a van and driven them off.

Clue 3

Danny and Gareth's dads were clearly getting caught up in an intense rivalry again. And they were competing over the best scooter, skateboard ... or BIKE! Perhaps one of them had stolen the twins' bikes for parts.

It was getting quite late. I looked up from my **CASE FILE** to stare pensively out of the window. A man in a **SPACESUIT** flew past my window on a skateboard and waved at me. I waved back. Then I realised that skateboards **DON'T FLY** and that men in spacesuits don't just float around the street. I looked out of the window again, but the spaceman had vanished. I *really* needed to get some sleep!

LOG ENTRY #7

Location: The roller rink
Status: Questioning everything

I scooted into town at around eleven

o'clock on Tuesday morning. Gareth had

asked to meet me by the roller rink, but he

hadn't said what he wanted.

I had two suspicions: either he knew

something about the missing bikes, or he wanted to ask Holly out and needed advice from her best friend. I had to tread carefully.

As I arrived, Gareth was walking out of Curly Greg's repair shop with a bag.

I stopped in my tracks: Gareth had his hair dyed red. Recently.

'Mina, you came!' Gareth looked pleased to see me.

'Hi Gareth!' I said. 'When did you get your hair done?'

'Err … Sunday night,' Gareth replied. 'My mum did it when I got back from the roller rink. Everyone is having it done. Just 17 do their hair like this. Do you like it?'

I didn't really know whether I liked it or not, but I didn't want to be rude. 'Yeah, it really suits you … What's in the bag?'

Gareth smiled, almost forgetting to answer my question. 'The bag? Oh! Yes! Just a couple of parts I ordered yesterday, to put the finishing touches to my scooter.'

'I'm sure it will look amazing' I said, trying to think about how to question Gareth about his dad without raising **SUSPICIONS**.

'Will your dad be entering?' I asked bluntly. 'It's just that I heard something about Danny's dad and your dad always competing.'

'Yes, I think so,' said Gareth, 'although he hasn't talked to me about it. He's usually quite secretive about his inventions.'

I felt like I may have hit a nerve. Gareth's dad is so competitive that he doesn't let anything get in the way of his **INVENTIONS**, not even Gareth. I must have looked awkward because Gareth quickly jumped in and changed the subject.

'How are you getting on with your scooter?' he asked me.

I looked down at it. Tinfoil and sticky tape were dragging along the floor, and had picked up old crisp packets and other bits of rubbish.

'It's not finished,' I clarified.

'Well …' said Gareth, 'if you want any help just let me know.'

I smiled. 'Thanks. Anyway, what did you want? You said it was **IMPORTANT**.'

Gareth looked really flustered. He was really struggling to say whatever he was going to say.

'Erm … you know dates?' he said finally.

I stared at him, confused. 'The ones you eat or the ones historical events happen on?'

Gareth looked down at his feet. 'Err … no, neither of those.'

I suddenly realised what was going on.

'Oh, this *is* about Holly!' I said. 'Yes Gareth, I'm sure she wants to go on a date with you.'

Gareth looked lost. 'No … but …'

'Sorry Gareth, is there anything else?' I asked impatiently. 'Only, my cousins' new bikes went missing and I'm looking for any information I can find. All that I know is that they were two new bikes, one red and one blue, and someone put them into a van and **STOLE THEM**.'

Gareth stopped stuttering for a minute. 'Well, I did see a van delivering two bikes, one red and one blue, yesterday ...'

This sounded promising! 'Oh wow! Where?' I asked him.

'Well, right here,' said Gareth. 'To Greg's skate and bicycle repair shop. Yesterday, when I came to order these parts, there was a **YELLOW VAN** at the back of the shop. Someone was unloading two new children's bikes from it: **ONE BLUE AND ONE RED**.

I was shocked. A yellow van, a red hair …

could it be Granny Meera??? My mind

went back to our conversation at the party,

when I was queuing for cake. I remembered

Granny Meera saying the Mayor was

organising mysterious grand prizes for the

winners of the two skate park competitions.

I also remembered hearing Dad say that the

Mayor couldn't organise his way out of a

paper bag …

What if the prizes had never

turned up? Could Granny Meera and

the Mayor have plotted to steal the bikes? It certainly looked that way.

The question was: **WHY?** Granny Meera is one of the nicest people in the world. For her to do something so terrible, there had to be an explanation. Maybe the Mayor had threatened to stop hiring her catering service. That could be a big blow for her business ... or perhaps she was in danger – maybe even **LIFE-THREATENING DANGER!**

I might have found out who had stolen
the bikes, but the case wasn't closed. Now I
needed to know why.

'Mina … Mina … sure you're **OKAY?** … **EARTH TO MINA** …'

I must have been in my own world for a while thinking all that. Suddenly I realised that Gareth had been trying to get my attention for a while.

I smiled distractedly at him. 'Gareth, sorry … yes. Thank you … sorry. I have to go …'

I jumped on my scooter and set off for **AUNTIE NAYNA'S HOUSE**, tin foil dragging on the floor and crisp bags blowing in the wind.

As I scooted away, I shouted back to

Gareth over my shoulder. 'Thanks Gareth …

And don't worry, I'll tell Holly about the date!'

LOG ENTRY #8

Location: My bedroom

Status: Making plans

I was really anxious as I rode to

Auntie Nayna's. The whole point of

me arranging this appointment with

her had been to **SECRETLY**

INTERROGATE her, to find

out if she knew anything about the missing bikes. Now I knew *where* the bikes were, but I still needed to know *why* the bikes had been stolen and *who* knew about it. This was going to be a delicate operation. If Auntie Nayna didn't know anything and I gave the game away, I could get a lot of people in trouble: the twins for disobeying her and leaving the garage unlocked, and GRANNY MEERA FOR STEALING.

I hadn't really thought about what I was going to say when I rang the doorbell, and it was too late by the time Auntie Nayna answered the door. She looked really happy to see me.

'**MiNA!!** Finally, you leave your hair in my hands. You won't regret this.'

I had a feeling I *was* going to regret this. Granny Meera left her hair in Auntie Nayna's hands **AND NOW SHE HAS A RED MOHiCAN**.

I put on a hopeful smile. 'Hi Auntie Nayna! Thanks for this, it's just a trim that I want though … nothing too crazy.'

Auntie Nayna shook her head at me. 'Now, I'll be the judge of that! Don't worry, I won't cut it short or anything like that. Now, where did I put **THE PURPLE DYE?**'

I decided it was time to launch into my casual interrogation. 'Isn't it terrible about the twins?'

'Oh Mina, it's just awful,' she said. 'They were **SO UPSET** about the festival.

But I've told them not to worry; there's other nice things to look forward to.'

I wasn't sure whether Auntie Nayna was unaware of the bikes going missing, or whether she was working with Granny Meera to cover up the theft. I seriously doubted Auntie Nayna had anything to hide. She had been away when the bikes went missing and, you know, she is their mum. I couldn't imagine her ever doing anything that could upset the twins.

I decided to be a bit more direct, just in case. 'Yes, like the bike park opening!

They must be looking forward to that, so

they can try out their new bikes, right?'

Auntie Nayna stopped what she was doing

and turned to look me straight in the eye.

'Mina, you're not just here for a snazzy haircut, are you?'

BUSTED!!!!!

'I know why you're here,' Auntie Nayna continued. 'You know your cousins are disappointed about the concert and you want me to use my influence as Just 17's make-up artist and hairdresser to get them to perform a surprise gig for the twins.'

How on earth did she come to that conclusion??!!

I tried to relax and keep acting natural.

'Err … yes???'

'Well, I can't promise anything, but I'll see what I can do.' She shot me a sudden serious look. 'Not a word of this to the twins though, okay? I wouldn't want them to be disappointed again.'

I nodded. 'Okay, Auntie Nayna.' At this rate I was going to start losing track of all the secrets I was meant to be keeping.

'Now,' said Auntie Nayna, 'which do you prefer: green or purple?'

I DIDN'T PREFER GREEN OR PURPLE.

I preferred my own hair as it was.

'Neither?'

Auntie Nayna reached for her brush. 'I'm hearing purple.'

I wasn't sure how successful my day had been as I scooted back through town, on my way back from Auntie Nayna's.

I had discovered that Granny Meera,

who I loved and trusted, was running a

SECRET CRIME RING.

Three quarters of my scooter was dragging

along the floor and picking up everything

in its path, and I now had purple hair. Well, it's not all purple – just the ends. I do kind of like it, actually. Anyway, I guess this proves Holly wrong for saying that there's nothing interesting about me.

And then I remembered: 'Holly … I have to tell her that Gareth wants to ask her out.'

It didn't bother me at all that Gareth wanted to go on a date with Holly. I knew she'd be **REALLY HAPPY**, and everyone enjoys giving their friends news that makes them happy. The only

part that seemed a bit unfair was that,
in return, Holly was going to list every
possible combination of every single item
she had in her wardrobe. She would also
tell me all the reasons why she should or
shouldn't wear them on a date, and my
brain might **MELT** and dribble out
through my ear.

Just as I was thinking about this, I
passed Curly Greg's bicycle repair shop.
I decided to sneak around the back and
have a look through the window.

I crept quietly around the back of the shop and climbed up onto a skip, so I could look through the rear window. There, in the middle of the workshop were the two bicycles: fully modified and ready to be used as prizes for the competitions.

I wouldn't let those bikes be given away, that's for sure. But I also needed to find out exactly what had happened and why. I was sure the bikes would be safe where they were until the day of the bike show. I just needed to make sure that they ended up **REUNITED** with their rightful owners.

Before making my way home, I decided to drop in on Granny Meera. An hour later I left again, now I knew exactly what was going on, **AND I HAD A PLAN**.

When I got home, I called Auntie Nayna's house and asked to speak to my cousins. Maheshwari took the phone.

'Hi!' I said. 'Listen, I forgot to ask you if you'll be going to the skate park opening on Thursday.'

'What does she want?' said Mahesh in the background.

'She wants to know if we're going to the opening of the skate park on Thursday,' Maheshwari replied.

There was a pause while Mahesh thought about it. 'I don't know, I don't really feel like it. It would have been more fun if we had **OUR Bikes**.'

'Yeah,' said Maheshwari, 'it would have been more fun if we had our new bikes.'

I know, I know … but please come. Don't worry; you're going to have to trust me. Just promise me you'll be there, okay?

Okay, we promise.

I hung up, then I went over to the fridge.

There was a note on the door saying:

Just nipped out to see a client, won't be late. Shepherd's pie in fridge. Love, Mum xx

Nice, shepherd's pie! I prepared a tray, with plenty of food for me and some crisps for Mr Panda. Then I picked up the house phone and went up to my bedroom. My next phone call was going to be to Holly. I just hoped I had enough food to get through the night!

LOG ENTRY #9

Location: My bedroom
Status: Writing up the case

On Wednesday, I had arranged to meet up with Danny and Percy to finish decorating our scooters.

After several days of scooting around the village with wires and sticky tape dangling from my scooter, I had managed to drag **QUiTe A LOT OF RUBBiSH** along with me. Percy and Danny examined the scooter.

'Interesting …' said Percy, walking slowly around it.

Danny pulled out his notebook and scribbled something down. 'Very interesting.'

'Do you think we can fix it?' I asked

'We can wrap a load of tin foil around it.' Danny showed me the diagram he had drawn.

I looked down at the garden and all the **RUBBiSH** in it. Then I looked back at my scooter. I had an idea.

'Actually, we may not have to fix it,' I told Danny and Percy. 'I think I've just come up with a winning idea. Hear me out ...'

We spent most of the day working on our **SCOOTERS AND COSTUMES**. I didn't know whether we were in with a chance of winning, but we were definitely going to make a **STATEMENT**.

The opening ceremony started at four o'clock on Thursday afternoon. There was a crowd of people waiting for it to open.

You could sense the excitement in the air. Everyone had gone to loads of effort to customise their bikes, skates, skateboards and scooters. Lots of people had dressed up too.

The atmosphere was brilliant, until Holly's mum pulled up with a bus full of students from the local college.

They all got off the mini bus carrying signs. Then Holly's mum got out a megaphone and started screaming:

Holly rolled up to me looking really
embarrassed.

'Should I even ask what your mum's up
to?' I asked.

Holly shrugged. 'You can, but I have no
idea what they're protesting about this time.'

'Also,' I asked, 'do you have any idea
why they're all wearing really **UGLY
BEAD NECKLACES**,

almost identical to the one I made, that

you gave to your mum?'

'Oh, yeah,' she smiled. 'You mean the

NECKLACES they all bought for

five pounds each?'

I stopped and stared at her. **'FIVE**

POUNDS?!'

'You should know. You made them,' Holly replied, breezily. 'Well, that's what I told my mother. I made them really.'

'FIVE POUNDS EACH?!'

I repeated.

'Yep,' Holly replied. 'Easiest two hundred pounds I've ever made.'

'TWO HUNDRED POUNDS?!' At that moment, my

brain caught up with my ears. I narrowed my eyes. 'Wait a minute, I think I should get some of that: you used my name and my original design after all.'

Holly thought about it for a bit. 'Well ... I don't have much left after buying this **OUTFiT**.'

I took a step back to admire the outfit:

a white leather jumpsuit with **GOLD**

SEQUINS and a pair of angel wings

sewn onto the back, and a gold halo … all

in keeping with her white roller skates with gold sequins and gold feathers.

'That is an impressive outfit,' I agreed reluctantly.

Holly gave a little shimmy. 'I know, right? Gareth will not be able to resist me in this.'

I gave her a pointed look.

'Anyway,' she continued, 'I don't have much money left after buying this outfit, but I say we reinvest it in beads and we can make the matching earrings and bracelets. We'll split the profit!'

I wasn't convinced. I didn't really feel like sitting around at Holly's making jewellery, especially with the threat of a date with Gareth looming. Just think of all the **OUTFiTS** Holly would want to try on! I looked at Holly dubiously.

'And I'll buy you an ice cream,' she added.

The ice cream did make the offer seem more appealing.

'Okay, deal,' I said.

Suddenly we heard the crackling of loud speakers

and turned our attention towards the front
of the crowd. There was a small stage at
the front gate and a ceremonial ribbon had
been placed across the entrance to the park.

The speakers hissed again and the noise completely drowned out the protestors.

The village mayor took the stage and everybody clapped.

'Ladies, gentlemen and children of Greenville,' the Mayor began. 'We're here today to celebrate the **GRAND OPENING** of our brand-new bike and skate park, which will be a **FANTASTIC ADDITION** to our town and will surely be appreciated by many of our younger citizens.

'As you know, we have arranged two contests today: one for the **BEST CUSTOM VEHICLE** and one for the **BEST RIDER**. So please fill in a form at the entrance if you want to take part. Don't forget, we'll also be awarding the coveted prize for Greenville's Annual Environmental Award!'

There was a bored murmur in the crowd. It's hard to get people interested in an environmental award when everyone is hyped up about a skate park.

179

'And now, to cut the ribbon,' he continued, 'please welcome a very well-respected member of our community, who has helped us all by putting his heart and soul into this project, as well as by **SUPPLYING THE COMPETITION PRIZES**. Let's have a big hand for Curly Greg!'

Everybody clapped and cheered as Curly Greg took the stage and waved.

The Mayor passed Curly Greg a giant pair of **SCISSORS** and he stepped up to the microphone.

'Dear citizens of Greenville, a lot of people have worked very hard to make today an extra special day. Please enjoy the entertainment, there will be a few **SURPRISES!** I hope this new skate park will bring the community lots of happiness for years to come.'

He placed the open scissors over the ribbon, and as he snipped it, he said:

Everybody cheered, then slowly the

crowd started trickling through the gate.

THE SKATE PARK WAS AWESOME!

There was a covered roller rink that linked to a bit with all sorts of tricks and jumps of varying difficulty.

At the edge of the park, there was a long table with all sorts of food and drink at one end. I spotted Granny Meera and winked at her. She gave me a massive grin and a thumbs up.

I saw Danny and Percy too and remembered that we had to go and put our names down for the **CUSTOM VEHICLE COMPETITION**.

I asked Holly if she was coming too and she looked me up and down. 'You're entering the competition? Dressed like that?'

'Not on my own,' I explained. 'With Danny and Percy.'

Holly looked over at Danny and Percy. They waved at her. She started backing

away like she didn't want to be seen with us.

'No, it's okay. Why don't you guys go and put your names down for the competition without me? I'm going to see if I can find Gareth. After all, he hasn't asked me out yet, so I'm just wasting this outfit.' With that, Holly skated off into the distance.

I went to queue up with Danny and Percy, to put our names down for the best custom vehicle competition. While we were there, I noticed that the Greenville Environmental Award was still taking entries, and I had an idea …

As soon as we finished, we made our way over to the area where the **BEST RIDER COMPETITION** was taking place.

It was really thrilling to watch. A lot of people had entered and I was impressed at how good some of the contestants were. The first contestant was Debra Derby. We all knew that she was pretty good on roller skates – she never takes them off – but I'd never seen her jump and do somersaults and back bends and the splits!

There was no way she could lose! A few

other kids competed after her on their

bikes, skateboards and scooters ... Then

things started to get a bit weird.

   The next contestant was Miss Quimby –

the teacher who is obsessed with doughnuts

– on a stunt bike. This wasn't something

any of us thought we'd ever see. I would

have expected someone as unathletic

as Miss Quimby to have a lot of difficulty

riding a stunt bike. But as it turns out, I

was totally wrong. My jaw dropped. She

sped over a jump and flew through the air,

landing on just her front wheel. Then she

did the splits over the handle bars in mid-air,

and after a couple of incredible double somersaults it was clearly all over for the rest of the competitors. My jaw dropped. Miss Quimby the doughnut muncher had completely annihilated the competition.

Only a couple of contestants went on

after Miss Quimby – she was just too hard

an act to follow.

Gareth Trumpshaw was the first

contestant to show off his customised

scooter. He had flashing lights, a police

siren, an automatic parking system (not sure how useful that is) and it could even make you a cup of tea (if you had your own cup ... and your own tea).

Gareth looked over at me to see my reaction, and I gave him a big thumbs up. I felt bad about the last time I'd spoken to him and accidentally reminded him that his father doesn't like him getting in the way of his **INVENTIONS**.

Next up was … Mr N. Trumpshaw. I assumed that was Gareth's Dad?

We all looked around, but we couldn't

see him. Suddenly a man in what looked

like a spacesuit flew towards the stage

on a homemade hoverboard. We could

not believe our eyes: Gareth's Dad had

managed to invent a working, flying

hoverboard! I looked over at Danny and

Percy and we were all thinking the same

thing: **PLEASE DON'T LET
US BE UP NEXT**.

A call came through on the speaker

system: 'Danny Dingle, Mina Mistry and

Percy McDuff.'

RATS.

We took the stage and stood there for

a bit with our customised scooters. By

"customised", I mean that I'd managed to

convince Danny and Percy to embrace the

rubbish theme and just cover their scooters

in bits of old rubbish, crisp packets, loose

wires, anything we could find really! The

audience did not look impressed.

Danny leaned over to me and whispered:

'I told you we should have gone with the fire theme.'

I walked towards the microphone and prepared to deliver my speech.

Friends, neighbours, citizens of planet Earth, you may be wondering why we have decided to decorate our scooters … and ourselves … with rubbish.

Danny looked at our outfits as if he had no idea what I was talking about.

'… you see,' I continued, 'picking up only the rubbish that we came across in our everyday surroundings, we've found enough to cover ourselves in it completely. We live in a world of waste, of buying unnecessary things. And a lot of these things end up in landfills, or being shipped off to developing countries … or in Danny's garden. So this is our statement, to say please, just think about the planet.'

Quite a lot of people started clapping, especially the ones that Holly's mum had invited.

I turned to look victoriously at Danny and Percy, when suddenly there was an **ALMiGHTY CRY**.

'The Trumpshaw twit has stolen my idea, where is he?!'

A man in a scrappy homemade spacesuit came tearing around the corner on some sort of out of control **BOUNCiNG SKATeBOARD**. Percy and I turned to look at Danny.

'That's your dad, isn't it?' said Percy.

Danny nodded grimly. 'Yep.'

'He's going to challenge Gareth's dad to

a duel, isn't he?' I said.

Danny nodded again. 'Yep.'

Danny's dad hopped up the steps on what

looked like Danny's old skateboard,

with bits of old microwave and

exercise bike

attached to

a rather

unsteady

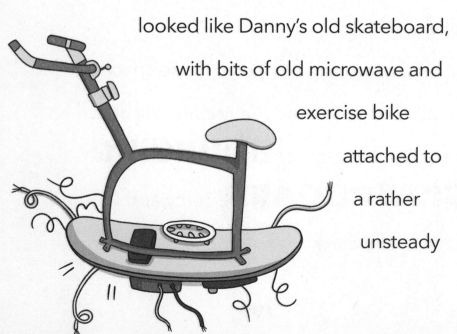

frame. Something in there was

WHiRRiNG and **CRACKLiNG**

as the contraption bounced up and down,

trying to stay in the air.

'Where is he?' roared Danny's dad. 'Neil

Trumpshaw!! Come back, I challenge you

to a duel!!'

I could see two security guards

making their way through the crowd.

It was at this point that Danny's dad's

hoverboard suddenly started overheating.

SPARKS started flying everywhere.

One of them flew into a crisp packet that

was hanging off Danny's scooter, which

promptly **CAUGHT FIRE**.

Danny stepped away from the scooter and a member of staff threw himself onstage, fire extinguisher in hand and started covering everything in foam.

I leaned over to speak to Danny. 'See? I told you that if we just used the tinfoil the fire would appear on its own, like it usually does.'

Danny and Percy both nodded in agreement.

We decided to leave the stage while Danny's dad was being escorted away by security … it was as good a time as any.

A few other people went up on stage to take part in the customised vehicle contest after us, but we decided we should probably go and find a quiet corner where we could take all the rubbish off our scooters before anything else **REALLY DANGEROUS** happened.

I was so distracted that I had almost completely forgotten the whole point of why I was there. That was until I heard the announcement:

Gather around everybody, we're about to announce the winners of the two competitions … But first, as a very special surprise, we have a special performance from everybody's favourite band … JUST 17!!!!!!

I leapt towards the stage, but wasn't quite fast enough. There was a loud scream as everybody registered what the Mayor had

just said and rushed to the stage. I had to
elbow my way through the crowd, but finally
I made it over to the wings. I could see the
whole audience from there, including Holly.
She was completely frozen, as if she couldn't
believe what she was seeing.

The band performed a few songs and ended it with their hit "Glowstick It".

When the band finished, Brent Lustly, the singer with the purple hair, went to the front of the stage and announced:

Thank you all for being here. Tonight, we're here to award two very special prizes … Not the prizes for the competition, but the prizes for the most patient twins in the world … Where are Mahesh and Maheshwari? Can you come up here?

I looked over and saw my cousins running towards the stage.

'Now, Mahesh and Maheshwari,' said Brent, once they had made their way up beside him, 'last weekend it was your birthday, wasn't it? Can you tell everybody what you got for your birthday?'

Mahesh spoke shyly into the microphone. 'Well, we were given two new bikes and tickets to see your concert in Rainy Valley.' Maheshwari nodded beside him.

'But the concert didn't end up

happening, did it?' the singer continued,

shaking his head sadly. 'The concert

was cancelled because of a mudslide,

and what should have been the best

weekend ever ended in **SOGGY**

DISAPPOINTMENT.

And then your strict parents forbade you from even riding your new bikes, didn't they?'

Mahesh looked like he was about to say something, but Maheshwari grabbed his sleeve and gave him a very pointed look before making an exaggerated sad face at the crowd.

'Isn't that the saddest birthday ever?' the singer called out to everyone.

'Awwwwwww!' replied the audience all together.

'When Mahesh and Maheshwari's mum told us what had happened, we just had to come and perform here to make it up to you. But there's another surprise waiting for you too …' The singer gestured off to the side of the stage. I turned to Granny Meera and nodded.

'You thought your parents were being super strict,' he continued, 'but you were very patient. I hear you didn't even complain once! Well, you didn't know that your family was working on an **EXTRA SPECIAL SURPRISE** for you behind the scenes. So, Mahesh and Maheshwari … **HERE ARE YOUR NEW BIKES!'**

At that moment Granny Meera and I wheeled the brand-new bikes onto the stage. They looked awesome! Granny Meera and Curly Greg had customised them with new suspension, flashing lights, Just 17 stickers … everything you can imagine!

The twins looked so excited I thought they were going to cry.

'So,' the singer concluded, 'Mahesh and Maheshwari, I hope this makes up for everything and that this is the **BEST BIRTHDAY EVER!**'

'Thank you, it is!' replied Mahesh and Maheshwari.

Once they had left the stage, Brent moved on to the next part of the announcements.

'And now, let's find out who the lucky winners are of the two competitions we've had here today – drum roll please. The winner of the best rider is …

Everybody held their breath.

'Miss Quimby! Miss Quimby, come up here and collect your prize. And the winner of the best customised vehicle is … Neil Trumpshaw!'

A distant cry of 'Noooooo!!!' was heard somewhere in the background. It sounded a lot like Danny's dad.

Gareth's dad and Miss Quimby took the stage. Shortly afterwards, Curly Greg and the mayor wheeled out their prizes: two fully customised children's bicycles.

Gareth's dad was the first to speak:
'Distinguished members of the community
… fellow skaters … I just want to say that I
worked really hard for this **PRIZE** and
that I won't be sharing it with anyone.'

He searched the audience and looked at Gareth intensely, then repeated, 'Not **ANYONE**.'

Gareth looked embarrassed and disappointed. I felt really sorry for him.

It was Miss Quimby's turn next.

Miss Quimby went up to the microphone. 'Err, yes. I just want to say to all the kids out there that I don't mind sharing my prize … with anyone who can catch me first!'

As everyone except the Mayor waved and left the stage, I looked around and couldn't help but feel that the kids weren't really getting the best deal. I mean, some of us had worked really hard on our vehicles. And when I say that, I'm referring to other people who made a bit more of an effort than gluing cola cans and crisp packets to their scooters and then writing a clever speech about trying to save the planet. I mean some **OTHER** people had really made an effort. It didn't seem fair that they would have to compete against adults.

The Mayor took the microphone again.

Well, that didn't turn out exactly as we had expected. I just thought I'd tell you that in the beginning, we were only going to let children under the age of 14 participate in the competitions.

But thanks to Lucille Loafer and her protest, we realised that age is just a number and that many adults act like children.

At this, the Mayor looked towards the back of the room at Danny's dad.

So in order to make everybody happy and to make sure that the skate park includes people of all ages, we have decided to make every Thursday and Sunday afternoon …

WAIT FOR IT …

Roller Disco Afternoon!

Miss Quimby, Gareth's dad, Danny's dad and about five other adults cheered and jumped up and down.

We all started moving away from the stage, but the Mayor called us back.

'If you'd all like to wait for a moment,' he said, sounding a little annoyed. 'It would seem that you're all forgetting about the grand prize for Greenville's Annual Environmental Award.'

Everyone in the crowd looked at each other. No one had really taken much notice of that. The Mayor continued:

'We haven't had many entries this year, in fact, we've only had one. But I can confidently say that our contestants are worthy of the **PRiZe**. So please give a big round of applause to Mina Snotbridge, Danny Dingle and Percy McDuff, and their moving speech about waste!'

Percy, Danny and I looked for each other in the crowd.

'Come on up here!' insisted the Mayor.

Percy, Danny and I made our way to the stage.

The Mayor leaned over the side of the stage, where someone handed him a box.

'And, the grand prize this year ...'

The Mayor handed me the box and we all looked inside it.

'It's a drone!' we all shouted at once. There was a big **'OOOOH!'** from the audience.

'I'll swap you' shouted out Gareth's dad.

Danny, Percy and I whispered to each other for a moment. Then Danny took the microphone from the Mayor and addressed the audience:

'Well, well, well … As you can see, we have a drone,' he said '… and we won't be sharing it with any adults who don't want to share their bikes.'

Neil Trumpshaw's face dropped and Miss Quimby blushed.

I took the microphone from Danny.

'But wait!' I shouted. 'We have decided that we could let the adults borrow the drone, to play with every Sunday evening, **iF**

they use it at the old roller rink and cancel

Sunday's disco afternoon at the skate park.'

At that, Danny, Percy and I descended the

stage. We'd have to wait for the adults to

come and negotiate with us.

I decided I'd go and talk to Gareth. He

looked like he needed cheering up. I found

him sitting in a corner, looking a bit glum.

'Hey,' I said.

Gareth looked up. 'Hey.'

I gestured to the edge of the skate bowl next to him. 'Can I sit here?'

Gareth shrugged. 'Sure.' He took a breath. 'Well done for getting the skate park back for us kids on Sunday evenings.'

'Thanks. We haven't finished the negotiations yet, but it's looking promising.' I hesitated for a bit, not knowing whether he'd want to talk about his feelings. 'Listen, I'm sorry about the thing with your dad …' I said.

'Thanks,' Gareth replied. 'It's okay. I don't take any notice anymore.'

'Well, anyway,' I continued. 'I think I can cheer you up.'

'Really?' said Gareth.

'Yeah … You know dates?'

'Yes …' Gareth looked at me beaming a hopeful smile.

'Well, you're going on one with Holly now …' I said cheerfully. 'Have fun!'

I got up and left as Holly rolled towards Gareth as fast as her skates could carry her.

I spotted Granny Meera putting out a tray
of baked bean onion bhajis and I went to
speak to her.

Hi Pumpkin! Fancy a plum
and fish finger samosa?

I glanced at the tray quickly. It looked a

bit dodgy. I decided to give it a miss.

Not right now thanks. Holly's
about to buy me an ice cream.
Have you seen the twins?

No sooner had I opened my mouth than
they appeared next to us.

'We'd like to talk to you, Mina,' said
Mahesh.

'In private,' added Maheshwari looking Granny Meera straight in the eye.

'Oh, I'll just go and talk to ...' Granny Meera didn't even bother finishing the sentence, she just wandered off out of earshot.

'So ...' started Mahesh.

'Who did it? What happened?' continued Maheshwari.

'Well,' I answered, 'it turns out that

NOBODY HAD STOLEN

your bikes. Your dad told you that he didn't want you to ride them until today because he had arranged for Granny Meera to pick them up and take them to Curly Greg's shop. That way, they could get them customised and give you a **BiG SURPRiSe**.'

Maheshwari looked at me suspiciously.

'Have you been in on it all along?' she asked.

It wasn't until I went round to Granny Meera's that I had found out what was really going on. I didn't like lying to my cousins. But on the other hand, I couldn't risk my cover being blown.

'Yes,' I lied, 'I was in on it all along.'

'But we thought that you were, you know ...**A PRIVATE DETECT**-'

I interrupted Maheshwari before she could finish.

'I know, I had to make you believe that so that you would ask me to find the bikes for you and not someone else.'

'OH!' exclaimed the twins in unison, happy with my explanation.

'Well thanks, Mina,' said Mahesh.

'You're welcome. Go and have fun on

your bikes.' I said, waving them off.

The twins wobbled off on their bikes as best they could, and Granny Meera came back over.

'All's well that ends well, Pumpkin,' she said, giving me a hug.

'Now', she said, 'go and have fun with your friends … I think that the disco is about to start.'

A shiver ran down my spine. I ran off to find Holly, Gareth, Danny and Percy. I could see them off in the distance, they all looked like they were heading for the front gate.

'Wait up, where are you going?' I called after them.

Danny turned around. 'Well, seeing as the grown-ups have taken over, we might as well take our drone and go and hang out at the roller rink.'

'Good idea,' I said, 'It won't be long before they're bored of this place.'

'You coming then?' said Percy.

I looked down at my clothes, 'I'm just going to pop home quickly to get changed, I'll see you at the roller rink,' I said. 'Save me some crisps.'

So here I am, finishing off my **CASE NOTES** with Mr Panda before I join everyone to play "Who can stuff the most crisps into their mouth in one minute?"

It has been a **VERY** strange week and a **VERY STRANGE INVESTIGATION**. I ended up investigating a crime that hadn't really been committed and now we finally have an adult-free place to hang out, and a brand new drone!

I just hope that we won't end up forgetting the simple things in life that we enjoy doing in our free time.

This is **MiNA MiSTRY** signing

off on another solved case.

LOOK OUT FOR MINA'S NEXT INVESTIGATION

MINA MISTRY

(SORT OF) INVESTIGATES

THE CASE OF THE SPOOKY NEXT DOOR NEIGHBOUR